Secret Santa

The Story of the Girl Who Saved Christmas

Megan Leach

Secret Santa

Secret Santa

THE NORTH POLE

You may think Christmas only has a father,
but you would be wrong.
I'm here to tell you that Christmas has a daughter,
and this is her song.

Samantha Claus grew up in Greenland,
just south of the North Pole.
She owned a reindeer farm,
and was only 11 years old.

You see, Samantha is the neice
of the man known as Kris Kringle.
She's the daughter of his sister,
and an elf named Jingle.

Samantha ran the farm
that raised magic reindeer.
The ones that pulled Santa's sleigh
for one night, every year.

You know Dasher and Dancer,
Comet and Blitzen.
But Sam knew their kids,
Neve and Nova, Whisper and Wicked.

One night, as Christmas approached,
Samantha was with her deer.
Jingle burst into the barn,
frantic, and without any cheer.

"What's the matter?" Sam asked.

"Why are you so pale?"

"Santa is sick!" Jingle cried.

"Christmas is cancelled!" he wailed.

Sam and Jingle rushed to the workshop
and found Santa with no joy.
He had a fever, and was too sick
to deliver gifts to good little girls and boys.

The elves closed the workshop.
And put the toys away.
They worried what the world would see
on the morning of Christmas Day.

At home that night,
Samantha laid in bed.
It was the eve of Christmas Eve
and thoughts raced in her head.

She worried about the good children
without presents under the tree.
She worried they'd think there'd been a mistake,
or that they'd been naughty.

When Christmas Eve came,
Sam hadn't slept a wink.
She knew she could save Christmas,
she just had to think.

Then she thought of it!
The perfect plan.
She could save Christmas,
it was in her hands!

Sam went to the barn and fetched her reindeer. Neve and Nova, Eagle and Dickens, Kieper and Halley, and Whisper and Wicked.

They were young bucks,
with button antlers on top.
Whisper was a doe,
and Neve still had spots.

Because they were still small,
they couldn't pull Santa's sleigh.
So Sam made a special sled,
just for Christmas Day.

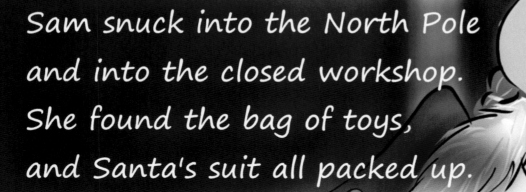

Sam snuck into the North Pole
and into the closed workshop.
She found the bag of toys,
and Santa's suit all packed up.

His boots were too big,
and she had to tie his belt real tight.
His jacket was too baggy,
and didn't fit quite right.

She made a beard from hair
that she borrowed from the cat.
But she felt the real power of Christmas,
when she put on Santa's hat.

She was a Claus after all,
Christmas was in her blood.
Then, Sam took the sack of toys
and put it on the sled with a thud.

The young reindeer took to the sky,
and landed on the roof of the first house.
Samantha slid down the chimney,
quiet as a mouse.

She filled all the stockings,
and left the perfect toys.
She ate the cookies and read notes
from the good little girls and boys.

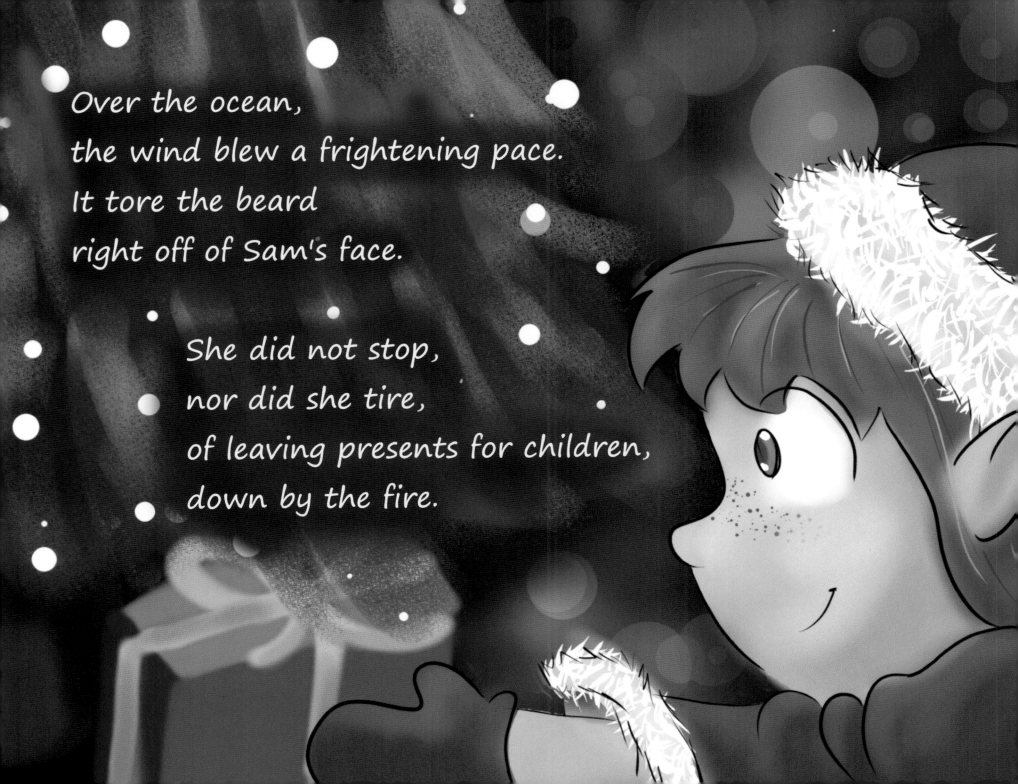

Over the ocean,
the wind blew a frightening pace.
It tore the beard
right off of Sam's face.

She did not stop,
nor did she tire,
of leaving presents for children,
down by the fire.

In one house, there was a noise
that left Sam startled.
In walked a little girl,
holding her bottle.

"Who are you?" she asked.

"I'm Santa," said Sam.

"No you're not," said the girl.

"Santa's a man."

Samantha frowned,
being put to the test.
She looked at the little girl,
pointed to her chest.

She said, "Santa's not just a man
who plays a part.
Santa's in all of us,
Because Christmas lives in your heart."

Sam gave the girl a candy cane,
and carried her to bed.
Then, she took off her hat,
and placed it on the girl's head.

Then she ran up the chimney
and took to the skies,
delivering the last toy
as the sun began to rise.

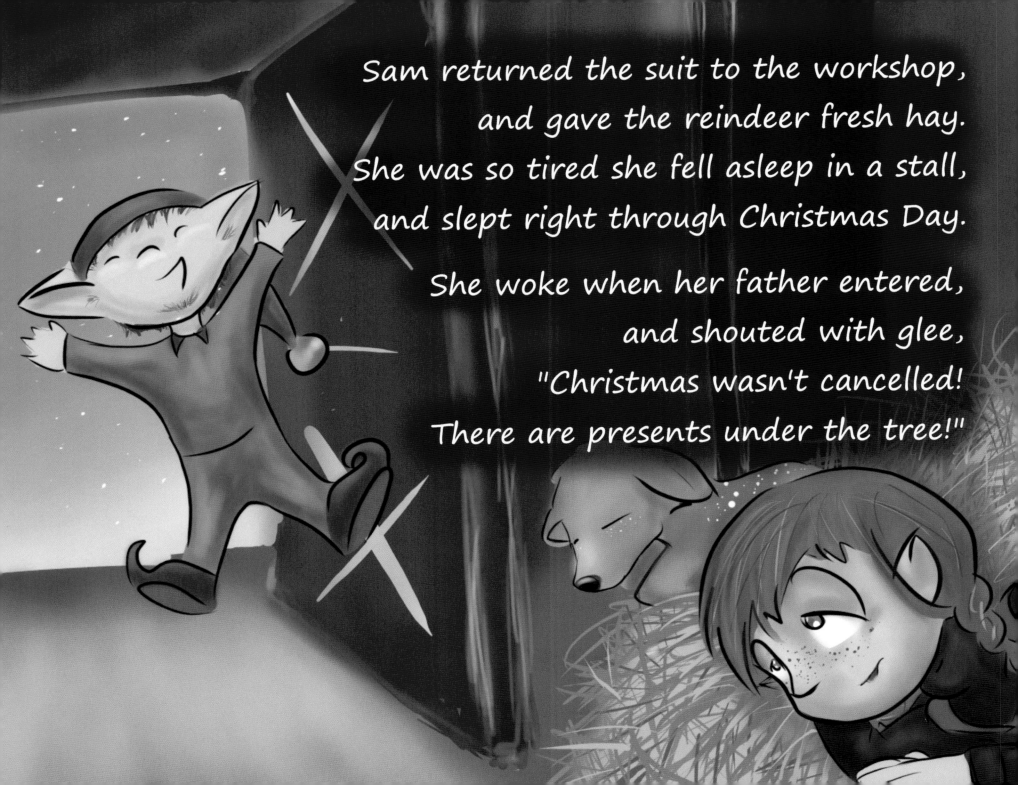

Sam returned the suit to the workshop,
and gave the reindeer fresh hay.
She was so tired she fell asleep in a stall,
and slept right through Christmas Day.

She woke when her father entered,
and shouted with glee,
"Christmas wasn't cancelled!
There are presents under the tree!"

There were presents for her mother,
and Jingle the elf.
But Sam had been so busy,
she'd forgotten herself.

Later that day,
a call came on the phone.
Santa invited Sam
to visit the North Pole.

When she arrived,
he was standing by the tree.
"You forgot something," he said.
"This one's from me."

She tucked her present under her arm.
Santa only smiled and sat.
"I have only one question," he asked.
"Where is my hat?"

"It's in the home of a girl," said Sam.
"Her name is Marceline."
"She saw me without a beard,
and I worried she wouldn't believe."

Santa smiled and nodded,
and walked his niece out.
He let her ride Blitzen
back to her house.

Back at the barn,
as Sam lay with her deer.
She unwrapped her package
of Christmas cheer.

The End

CPSIA information can be obtained at www.ICGtesting.com
Printed in the USA
BVIW120238051120
592596BV00006B/12

* 9 7 8 0 5 7 8 7 5 6 7 4 5 *